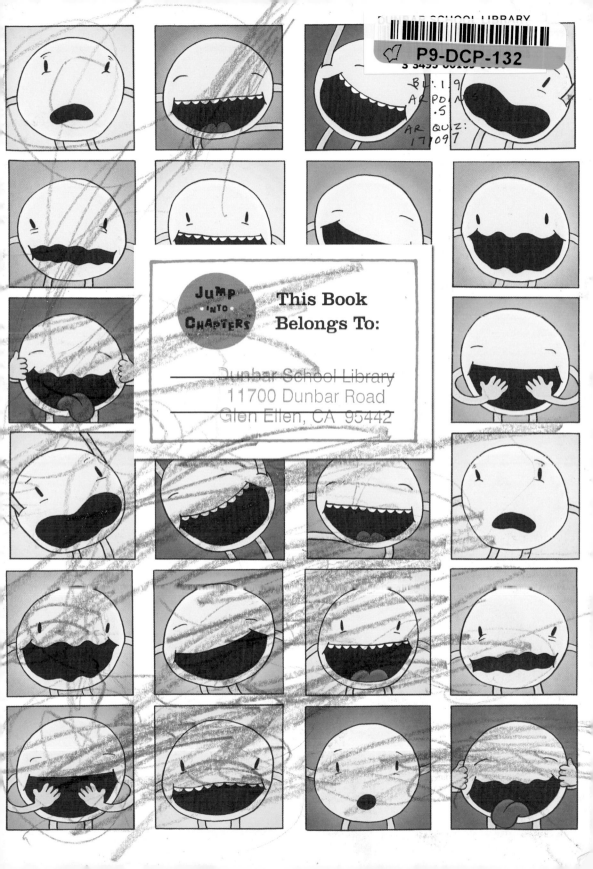

A **Jump•into•Chapters** Book™

Copyright © 2014 Michael Townsend
All rights reserved/CIP data is available. Published in the United States 2014 by
Blue Apple Books, 515 Valley Street, Maplewood, NJ 07040
www.blueapplebooks.com
First Edition 09/14
Printed in China
ISBN: 978-1-60905-458-8 (hardcover edition)
ISBN: 978-1-60905-554-7 (paperback edition)

2 4 6 8 10 9 7 5 3 1

MR. BALL

an EGG-cellent Adventure

Michael Townsend

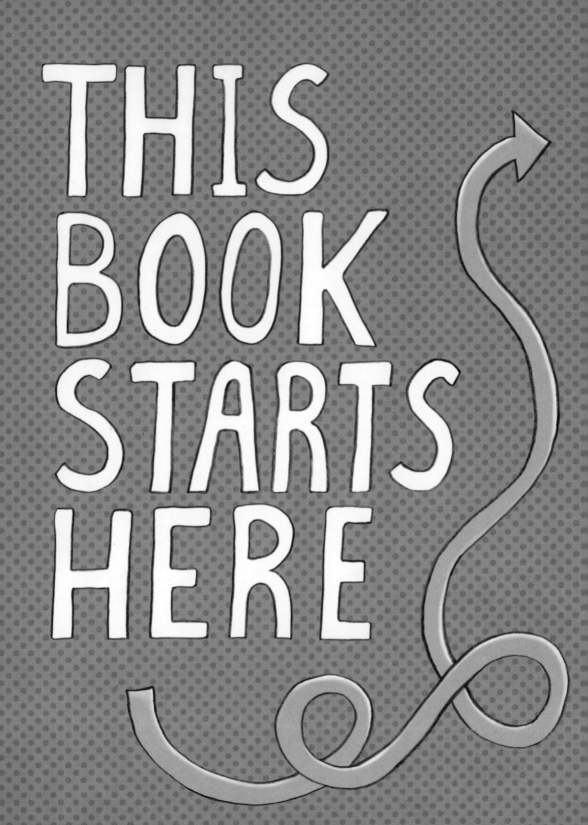

Part 1.
STARTS
HERE

PART 1.

Mr. Ball has a Wild and Scary Idea

Mr. Ball is going to the circus.

He is excited to see the big, wild, scary animals.

Even the high-flyers
did not thrill
Mr. Ball.

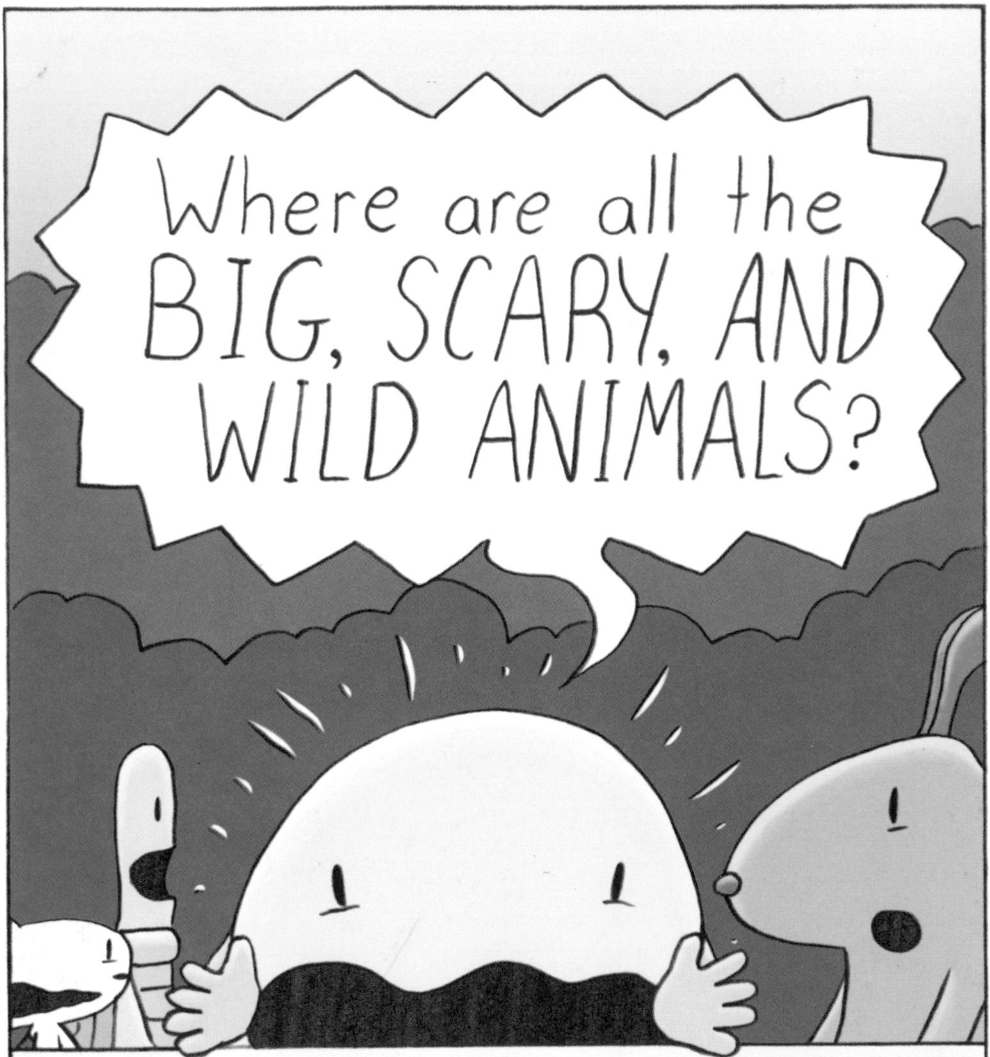
Where are all the BIG, SCARY, AND WILD ANIMALS?

Suddenly...

Mr. Ball roared with joy for the rest of the show.

I will do a clown act!

I will do a high-flying act!

Part 2.
STARTS
HERE

PART 2.

Mr. Ball is Warned

But I want a big, wild, and scary animal!

I'm warning you, Mr. Ball.

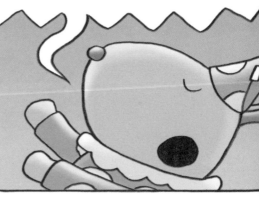

I once tried to have a **BIG PET.**

I once tried to put a dress on a wild, scary wolf.

What happened?

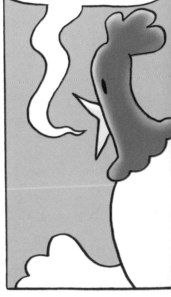

He didn't like it.

Part 3.
STARTS
HERE

PART 3.

A Big, Scary, Wild Plan

Step 1: Find a beast.

Step 2: Catch it.

Step 3: Tame it.

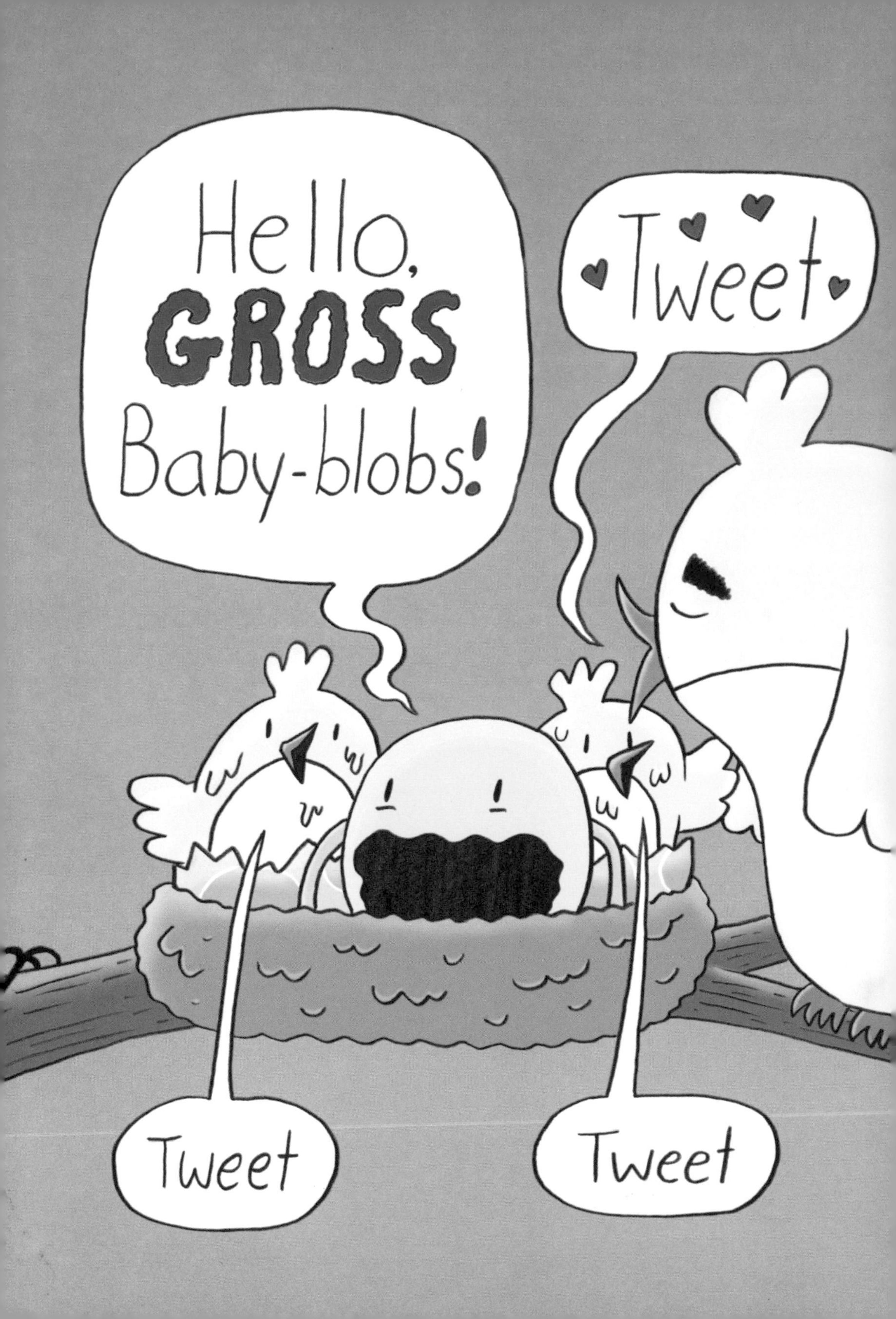
Hello, GROSS Baby-blobs!
Tweet
Tweet
Tweet

Hmmm... your Mama is large, but you guys are small!

I have a new plan!

First, I will tame you. Then, you will get big and giant.

Mr. Ball's new plan was off to a bad start...

If only he could fly like a bird.

Sadly, he was not a bird, but did the Mama-Blob know this?

Mr. Ball quickly got back in the nest.

He then did his best to blend in with the mini-blobs.

Things got worse for Mr. Ball when dinner arrived.

He was pretty sure he would not like having chewed up worms fed to him.

He was right!

Mr. Ball was trapped, scared, and **SOOO** not hungry.

Part 4.
STARTS
HERE

PART 4.

Mr. Ball Needs Help!!!

Oh my! Mr. Ball is stuck in a tree and needs our help!

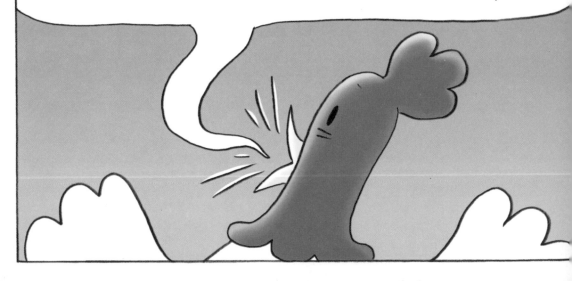

They raced through the woods. But would they be too late?

When they arrived...

The Mama bird is teaching her babies to fly!

VROOOOM

A short time later, Mr. Ball was cooking up some hot dog

I still want to tame a large scary animal.

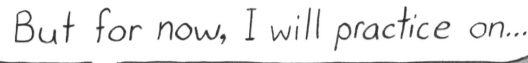

But for now, I will practice on...

My crazy little lion-kitty.

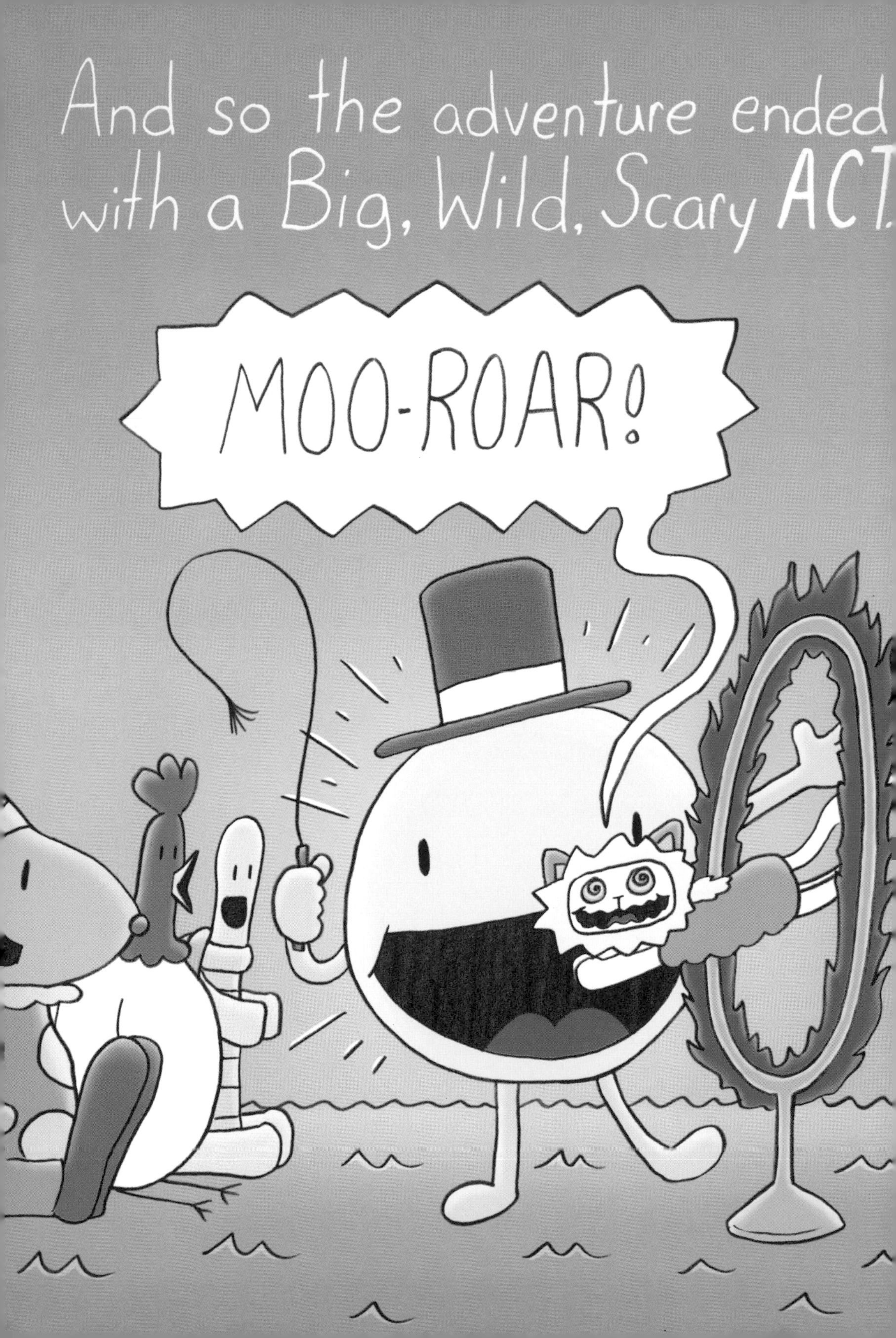
And so the adventure ended with a Big, Wild, Scary ACT.
MOO-ROAR!

THE STORY ENDS HERE

Join us next time when we find out if Tweety Blobs like pie...

Just kidding, the next book will be about Mr. Ball.

But in case you are wondering, Tweety Blobs **do** like pie!

A few seconds later...

THIS BOOK ENDS HERE

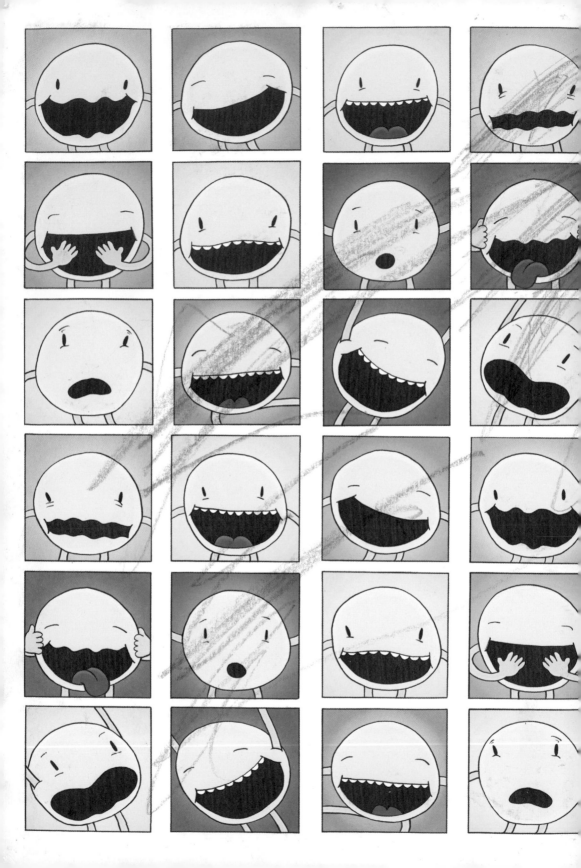